Written by
AMBER HARRIS

Illustrated by
ARD HOYT

To Justin, Tanner, Jake, and Teagan
—Amber

To my uncle Richard Hansen, with admiration
—Ard

Published by Redleaf Lane
An imprint of Redleaf Press
10 Yorkton Court
Saint Paul, MN 55117
www.RedleafLane.org

First edition 2015
Book jacket and interior design by Jim Handrigan
Main body text set in ITC Bookman Std Light

Manufactured in Canada
22 21 20 19 18 17 16 15 1 2 3 4 5 6 7 8

Library of Congress Control Number: 2015900872

My name is
Wisteria Jane Hummell.

My momma named
me Wisteria on account
of wisteria being her
most favorite flower.

She said, "Wisty Jane, I named you after the most beautiful flower I'd ever seen, because you were the most beautiful baby I'd ever seen."

Sometimes Momma says she should have named me Trouble. I sure am glad she didn't do that, because Trouble is not a good name.

I have looked at my
baby pictures, and
Momma is right
about me being
a beautiful
baby.

The
HUMMELL
FAMILY

One day I was playing with my friend Ella Darby and got to wondering what *her* baby pictures might look like.

“Yikes!” I said when she showed me, because Ella was a wrinkly mess.

But then I got to thinking maybe
Ella is what her momma calls
her on account of Ella's real
name being Elephant.

I have seen baby elephants at the zoo, and they are a wrinkly mess.

I told Ella why I thought her name was maybe Elephant.

Ella yelled, “My name is not Elephant, and I was not a wrinkly mess! Your name should be Monster, because you’re so mean!”

Next thing I knew, I was home, and Mrs. Darby told Momma just what I'd done.

Momma said, “Wisteria Jane, do you understand why Ella’s upset?” I was so glad she asked, because I surely did not.

She said, "Wisty, when you say
mean things to your friends,
you hurt their feelings."

Well, now I was confused. “Momma,” I said. “I didn’t say anything mean to Ella. You said I always need to tell the truth, and that is just what I did.”

Momma said,
"Wisty, you do
need to tell the
truth, but if something
might hurt someone's
feelings, you should think
twice before you say it—and
maybe even keep it to yourself."

I told Momma, "I am good at
keeping things to myself."

"I never told a single person about the time Daddy broke your favorite teacup."

"And I never did tell you that Bingo wet on your bed. I kept that one all to myself."

I told Momma, "I got so many think-twice thoughts up in my head, a few more sure won't be a problem."

Momma chuckled and gave me a hug. Then she took me into the kitchen and made me an ice cream cone, which was a bit surprising. But I just ate that ice cream and talked to Momma some more about thinking twice and being nice to people's feelings.

"I ought to draw Ella an apology picture," I said to Momma. I drew a rainbow unicorn. Unicorns are my favorite animals, and rainbow is my favorite color.

Momma walked me back over
to Ella's house to deliver my
"I am so sorry I said you look
like an elephant" picture.

Ella

Ella made a stink-eye face at me to let me know she was still very mad.

I said, "Ella, I am sorry I said a mean thing about your baby pictures. I colored you a nice apology, because I don't want you to be mad. I promise to tell my mouth not to say all the things my brain thinks."

Ella said, “Thanks, Wisteria. I really like the unicorn, and rainbow really is my favorite color.”

Well, my mouth wanted to tell Ella that rainbow was
my favorite color and that she was just a big old copycat.

But then I got to thinking maybe this would be a good time to keep my not-so-nice thought to myself. I took a deep breath, and I blew it out real slow. I said, "You are welcome, Ella. I also love rainbow."

"Maybe that is why we are such good friends."